DISCARD

P9-DMO-459

7-01
431226-01
OCT 2003
49-2
JUL 2003

First published in Switzerland under the title *Kleiner Eisbär kennst du den Weg?*

First published in the United States, Great Britain, Canada,
Australia, and New Zealand in 1996 by North-South Books,
an imprint of Nord-Süd Verlag AG, Gossau Zürich, Switzerland.
Distributed in the United States by North-South Books Inc., New York.
Library of Congress Cataloging-in-Publication Data is available.
A CIP catalogue record for this book is available from The British Library.
ISBN 1-55858-630-X (trade binding)
1 3 5 7 9 TB 10 8 6 4 2
ISBN 1-55858-631-8 (library binding)
1 3 5 7 9 LB 10 8 6 4 2
Printed in Belgium
For more information about our books, and the authors and artists
who create them, visit our web site: http://www.northsouth.com

Little Polar Bear, Take Me Home!

Written and Illustrated by

Hans de Beer

Translated by Rosemary Lanning

North-South Books
New York / London

Lars, the little polar bear, lived at the North Pole, surrounded by ice and snow. One day Lars sat staring at the ocean.

"I'm bored," he growled. Then his stomach growled too. "And hungry," he added.

Lars decided to go and explore the dump behind the polar research station. He knew he would find something good to eat there, and watching the seagulls soaring over the dump was more interesting than watching waves go endlessly up and down.

20

Lars found two chicken drumsticks and a few other tasty looking scraps and carried them across to the railway siding, where he could eat in peace. He spread out his feast and started to eat. But when he reached for the chicken, it wasn't there! Where had it gone?

Lars peered inside the train. A strange striped animal stared back. A piece of chicken fell out of its mouth. Lars gaped in astonishment.

The striped animal started to cry.

"Who are you?" asked Lars.

"I'm Sasha and . . . and . . . I'm so hungry."

"Hello, I'm Lars," said the little polar bear. "Have some more to eat, and tell me what you're doing here."

"Well," Sasha began, with his mouth full, "my father has often told me about the ocean at the end of the railway track. He says there's nothing finer in the whole world."

"Does he really?" asked Lars, rather surprised.

"Yes, and I've always wanted to see it. I thought this train might take me there. So I climbed inside and I rode for such a long time. But I didn't see the ocean and now I'm lost and scared and tired and I just want to go home!" Sasha started to cry again.

"Don't be scared, Sasha," said Lars. "I've often been far away from home, and sometimes I got a bit lost too. But someone always helped me get back, and now I'll help you. Why don't you take a nap first? I'll keep watch." But no sooner had Sasha fallen asleep than Lars nodded off too.

Suddenly the door of the train slammed open with a loud bang. Lars and Sasha woke with a start. They hid behind a stack of crates while more crates were loaded and didn't dare come out until the train started moving.

"We could be in luck," said the little polar bear, sounding braver than he felt. "You may be on your way home already."

They climbed onto the crates and looked outside.

"Where are we?" asked Sasha anxiously.

"We're . . . um, um . . . I don't know," Lars confessed.

Neither of them spoke again for a long time.

ЛОМОНД
СОЛНЦЕ НОЧЬЮ!

Slowly the view outside changed.

"Look, Lars," cried the little tiger. "Trees! This looks like home! Quick, let's get off!"

"We'll have to jump," said Lars. He waited for the train to slow down, then he climbed out of the window.

Sasha didn't look quite so eager now. "Can't we wait until the train stops?" he said.

"Come on, Sasha," Lars shouted. "You can do it!"

They tumbled off the train and rolled through deep, soft snow.

The little tiger sniffed the air. "Yes, it definitely smells like home," he said happily.

Which way now?" asked Lars.

Sasha didn't know. "I can't find exactly the right scent," he said.

A huge snowy owl swooped down and landed in front of them. "What are you looking for?" she asked.

"Sasha wants to go home," said Lars.

"He's still got a long way to go," hooted the owl. "Follow the railway tracks as far as the bridge. Then turn off, into the forest. After that, just follow the sun. Good luck!" She soared away.

"What a helpful owl!" said Lars.

"Rather big and scary," said Sasha. "Do you think we'll find the way now?"

"Of course," said Lars.

They reached the bridge, turned into the forest and followed the sun, which they could just see between the trees. They stopped when they came to a stream. Sasha was afraid to cross it.

"I'll help you," said Lars. "I'm used to water."

Then it began to snow, harder and harder. Soon a blizzard was blowing into their faces. They had to close their eyes and feel their way forward. Sasha began to whimper.

"All right," said Lars. "We'll stop and take shelter until the storm passes."

By morning the storm had died down, and when the sun broke through the clouds, Lars and Sasha found they had spent the night at the edge of the forest. A huge, empty plain stretched out in front of them.

"Which way now?" said Lars, under his breath, hoping the little tiger wouldn't hear.

"Are you gentlemen lost?" they heard a friendly voice say.

Lars and Sasha turned and saw a strange animal with two humps.

"Hello. I am Kasim. Shall I carry you across the plains?"

"Yes, please!" cried Lars, and they quickly clambered onto Kasim's back.

"Hold on tight," said Kasim. "Here we go, to Tigerland!"

Near the end of their long ride, Sasha grew more and more excited. He lifted his nose to the wind and wriggled impatiently. Suddenly he jumped down. "Home!" he cried, and ran off.

Lars and Kasim laughed.

"Thank you, Kasim," said Lars hurriedly. "Come and visit me at the North Pole one day." Then he ran to catch up with Sasha.

When they came to the edge of a tall cliff, Sasha scampered across a log bridge.

Lars looked down at the water rushing over the rocks below.

"Er . . . maybe we should find another way across," he said nervously.

"That would take much too long," Sasha called over his shoulder. "Come on, Little Polar Bear, you can do it."

By the time Lars had crossed the bridge, Sasha was way out in front and Lars could hardly keep up with him.

"Hey, little bear," called a woodpecker. "Watch out. This place is crawling with tigers. It's not safe for . . . "

Lars heard a rustle. He turned to find two enormous tigers standing in front of him. Then he saw Sasha and sighed with relief.

"Mama, Papa, this is my friend Lars."

"H-hello," stammered Lars. His heart was still thumping.

"Don't worry, Little Polar Bear," said Mother Tiger. "We won't hurt you."

When Sasha and Lars told Father Tiger about their adventure, he smiled at the little polar bear. "Thank you for your help, Lars. Now I'll take *you* home. Sasha can come with us."

"Great! Then I can show him the ocean. I know a really good place to sit and watch the waves," said Lars.

The homeward journey was much faster, because Father Tiger didn't lose his way as Lars and Sasha had done.

When at last they got back to the North Pole, Lars proudly showed them the ocean.

"There's nothing finer," said Father Tiger, while Sasha stared in amazement at the endless expanse of water.

"There you are at last, Lars!" called Lars's father.

Lars ran up to him. "Come and meet my friend Sasha," he said.

Father Tiger and Father Polar Bear soon became friends too.

Then it was time to say good-bye.

"Come back soon!" said Lars.

"I will, now that I know the way," said Sasha.

Lars waved until the tigers disappeared over the horizon.

Since then Lars has never felt bored watching the ocean. Often he murmurs to himself, "There's really nothing finer."